Introduction

Chalk Circle is a group of Sussex-based writers producing fiction for publication. We meet regularly to discuss progress on individual work and to collaborate on joint writing projects.

Strata is our first venture into microfiction, short works of 350 words or less, reflecting the variety of styles and interests within the group. From fatal attractions to tales of triumph and despair, broken hearts and hopeful ones, these stories represent fragments in time: slices through the human landscape.

For further copies of this anthology or for news of other Chalk Circle publications, competitions and events, visit www.chalkcircle.org.uk

STRATA

Slices through the human landscape

Microfiction by

Jayne Block · Judith Bruce · Stuart Condie
Yvonne Hennessy · Samantha Munasing · Danielle Sensier

Edited by

Danielle Sensier

Chalk Circle

Published in the United Kingdom by Chalk Circle, 2018
www.chalkcircle.org.uk

Copyright © Chalk Circle, 2018

Front Cover Illustration copyright © John Vernon Lord, 2018

Inside Illustration copyright © Tashi Reeve, 2018

The stories have been reproduced with the permission of the authors

A catalogue record for this book is available from the British Library.
ISBN 978-1-9164488-0-3

Acknowledgements
Chalk Circle writers would like to thank Catherine Smith and Jon Walter for their encouragement; the support of Zef Productions Ltd and The Depot, Lewes, our regular ever-friendly meeting venue.

Contents

Selkie

Yvonne Hennessy

A sea-fret rolled in; with each new wave it billowed across the sand till it lingered just below the footpath, shrouding pebbles, rocks and fishing boats, even threatening to seep further into the village. And as the sun rose in the east, its rays hovered above the mist like a thrown scarf of silken threads.

A small humped body wallowed at the water's edge, wet, grey skin reflecting flashes of silver as it twisted and turned through the foam.

From around the bay the other creature came, companion to the mist, its single horn pierced the dawn light. As it reached the spot where the seal lay - exhausted now - at the fringe of sea and beach, it stopped, lowered its long head and nudged the blubbery body, rolling it over and over through the froth, again and again.

Slowly the grey skin peeled away, first from the seal's head, releasing long tresses of dark hair, then revealing the face of a girl. The creature licked the seal's upper body, like a mare freeing her foal from its birth sac, until arms emerged and the girl was finally able to liberate herself. Stepping out of the remnants of her skin, she stood, waves bubbling around her ankles, and wound her arms around the creature's firm neck. She rubbed his muzzle, felt the soft fur of his mane run through her fingers and pressed her cold body close to his.

He nuzzled her hair, her cheek and her chest, but as he did so his horn began to dissolve, in minute trickles at first, then rapidly, like a melting icicle of mercury.

Once the fog had lifted two fishermen came down for their boats, lugging repaired nets and crab pots. The older one picked up the crumpled sealskin, held it for a moment as if weighing something in his mind, and then threw it back into the waves. The younger one called his father to where he stood, puzzling over a small pool of liquid silver by the tideline.

The Little White Dog

Stuart Condie

'*Qu'est-ce que tu fais là?*' she asked, squinting as the sunlight cast shadows across her face. A little white dog pulled on the lead she was holding.

I got off my bike and kicked out the stand, trying to marshal my recently completed GCSE French.

'*Je suis perdu,*' I replied with what I thought was a good Gallic shrug. I wasn't lost though; after the last argument with my father I'd ridden away to the lake to let off steam and knew how to get back. It wasn't his fault that Mum had left us; she'd just found someone else more exciting I suppose, though she might have thought more about those she'd left behind. My sister got on better with Dad, I just found him annoying.

'Ah, English,' she said and laughed. The dog barked twice as though agreeing with her. 'Lots of you *en Bretagne, pour les vacances.*'

'*Oui,*' I replied, entranced by her incense-like aroma.

She brushed an imaginary insect off her golden arm and lit two cigarettes, one for her, one for me.

I mumbled a *merci* and took a few puffs where her lips had just been. The dog pulled at his leash and scrabbled his legs. I bent down and stroked him, lucky animal.

'My parents come here every year, to the *manoir.*' She flicked her cigarette towards a large stone house over her shoulder. 'It's boring, just us and Fifou.'

'*Je suis aussi avec mes parents, dans une gîte.*' I sounded like a posh twat and felt myself going red. I got out my mobile to ask for her number.

'*T'a pas une bagnole?*' she asked, motioning a steering wheel after I'd looked blank.

I shook my head.

'*T'es trop jeune pour moi.*' She dropped her cigarette and twisted her foot over it. 'I thought you were older.'

As she kissed me on both cheeks her hair flicked into my eyes. 'Nice accent,' she whispered before walking off towards the stone house, Fifou running beside her.

I raced away on my bike to cool down. A real French girl had kissed me!

Fantasy

Samantha Munasing

One afternoon when I was almost fourteen we went to the cinema. The queue for tickets stretched along the foyer and out into the fiery day. Thathi had pre-booked the tickets so we headed for the bar. He ordered a whisky while Ammi made her face stony and refused a drink. I had an icy cold Coke and pretended it was whisky. Later in the theatre, the soft lighting hid the fraying velvet and made the fading silk curtains look grand, opulent.

A boy, perhaps seventeen or eighteen sat in the row in front. Thathi and Ammi were having a tense conversation. Ammi hated the smell of whisky. The boy glanced my way over his right shoulder. His eyes glittered like black jewels. He was dressed in untrendy clothes. A white shirt and pale cotton trousers. A small Afro drew attention to high cheekbones and face. I watched him out of the corner of my eye through the first half.

During the interval Thathi stumbled out, ignoring Ammi's venomous hissing. Luckily, the object of my attention had left too and so didn't witness this embarrassing episode. When he returned he glanced my way again, I remember that.

After the film I saw him at the bus stop when we passed by in the car. Our eyes collided and shut out Thathi and Ammi's sniping for a long moment. I made up a whole history for us, the first in my class to have a boyfriend. The other girls mostly envied me, but a few called me a slut.

Today when Mary visited with the baby she thought I was vacant. 'Mummy,' she said, her soft eyes crinkling with concern, 'Are you ok?' I smiled and reassured her but really, I wanted to be alone. My best moments are remembering him, glancing over his shoulder at me. Eyes like polished ebony. Sometimes a shiver scampers up my spine. I know then that right at that moment he is thinking of me too.

The Little Prince

Judith Bruce

She called him her 'Little Prince' - her only child, born when she was 47 years old. Yes. Amazing. As she would say 'I'd almost given up hope.'

Hope of what, though? She was a single parent and it was a struggle. Had the twenty-minutes of ecstasy with the sexy driver in the bus-garage that night been worth it?

Yes, yes - a thousand times yes. She had her 'Little Prince'. All the same, things weren't easy.

'He *is* my Little Prince, but it really is a struggle,' she would sigh. Was being a mother all that she had hoped for? Yes and no, was the answer. Mostly it was. But he was a bit of an odd one. That was the trouble. Not like other children. Didn't make friends. He didn't start to speak until he was five years old. Then they made him see specialists of course. Busy-bodies. Turned out he had - what was it? Begins with an 'a'. Alzheimer's? No. Asperger's. That was it. Funny names these medics give things.

He got passions. Obsessed with tadpoles at the moment. Collected them in a jar from the village pond on his way home from the Special Unit at his school.

I want to BE a tadpole, Mum,' he would say. "I want to understand how a tadpole actually feels.' Yesterday he had eaten one. Popped it into his mouth, chewed and swallowed it. 'Tastes like liquorice, Mum,' he said. 'Not sure that is a good idea, Little Prince,' she had said.

She was taking him a mug of cocoa that evening. Knocked on his bedroom door. Silence. She opened the door. The room was empty.

'Where are you, my Little Prince?' she asked.

The tadpoles were swimming around in their jar, and on the keyboard of his computer sat a frog. New-born. Tiny. Perfect in every detail.

'Here, Mum,' said the little frog.

Valerie

Danielle Sensier

Valerie lies face down on the recliner, enjoying the scent of newly-oiled skin and the lightness of her new silk two-piece. She has a boyish look: cropped hair, neat breasts, athletic limbs.

Feel the quality, not the width, Adam liked to say.

'Auntie *look*...' Sonny shouts, 'watch me jump!'

Valerie yawns. How many times can a small child jump in and out of a pool without getting bored? She doesn't know. Valerie never pretended to understand children.

Gouged from the dry mountain soil and edged with creeping grass, the swimming pool is her husband's pride and joy, his jewel; he loved to watch her swim in it. Miguel, the pool boy, kept a list of maintenance instructions in his apron pocket, just so Adam could see him tick it off.

'Auntie *see*... I'm floating.'

Valerie moves onto her side, turning away towards the patio, where Adam is entertaining their guests. He opens another bottle of vermouth, making a big performance about going to find more ice.

His relatives always were a thirsty lot.

The two sisters have forgotten their siesta voices: 'No, he didn't meet her *here* - it was some little club in Chelsea, apparently.'

'Probably a gold digger.'

'*Shh*... she'll hear you,' says the older one, stealing a look towards the pool.

Water splashes the back of Valerie's legs. 'Auntie... *please*...' She shakes it off, folding herself into a tight curve.

Everyone on the patio's whispering now, leaning into each other's necks like birds... until Adam returns, and they moved towards him again, laughing loudly, glasses raised.

'Auntie... auntie... *help!*'

Valerie often wonders about what happened next; her body slicing through the water . . . Sonny's weight in her arms, his flailing lungs . . . matchstick legs wrapped around her thighs.

And why no-one noticed sooner he was in trouble.

That giant rubber ring Adam bought him must have fooled them all - even the child's mother forgot he couldn't swim.

Still Life

Yvonne Hennessy

Three oranges lie in a bowl on the table; a black cat is curled nearby and beside the cat is an unopened brown envelope.

Opposite, against the wall there's a single bed; blankets cover a slight mound and dark hair tumbles across the pillow. From a plastic container above her head, a clear tube snakes down into the girl's nose.

The cat stands, stretches and settles down on the envelope.

Rain streams across the window and a dull, shadowless light seeps through the glass, along with the muffled buzz and thrum of the world beyond. The girl's mother sits by the window watching, waiting for the slightest movement; her daughter's breathing, still barely perceptible, is at least regular now. She crosses the room.

'Aisha, my love, it's time for lunch.' Leaning over, she embraces the crumpled body, whispering in her daughter's ear, 'look, naughty Minou's asleep on the table again.' The cat's tail flickers.

'Listen sweetheart, he's purring.' She opens the feeding tube valve: 'Your favourite today, Aisha - vegetable soup.' Green liquid moves down through the tube.

'Minou will be so happy when you're well enough to play with him.'

She perches on the side of the bed, twisting and untwisting the tail of a brown felt mouse, and running through yet again the Doctor's visit the previous day. In spite of his reassurances, how could she not worry?

His bulk had seemed to fill the tiny flat, but his voice was soft and slow. The young Syrian interpreter explained they'd seen many children like Aisha, children with Resignation Syndrome, children in shock:

She simply needs time to get over all you've been through.

The interpreter's expression acknowledged their shared experience.

If your residency here is confirmed, Aisha should gradually recover. Others have.

The mother clung to those words, like the few precious items salvaged from her ruined home. At the table, she finally slides the envelope from beneath the sleeping cat. The animal, disturbed, leaps down, strolls across the room and jumps onto the windowsill; a misty patch forms on the glass.

The Dog's Bollocks

Jayne Block

The news programme shows a boat bobbing on the freezing water, crammed with dark frightened faces that speak of unimaginable terrors.

Geoffrey watches the television in his drawing room. He sighs, throws another log on his fire and gives it a good stoke. Geoffrey's dog lies in its bed, beside the fire.

A politician calls for stricter quotas on the number of refugees Britain is expected to take in.

'Quite right,' mutters Geoffrey. 'I mean they can't speak a word of English Anne, can they?' He looks around, but his wife is not there. 'I don't know how they expect to fit in here,' he grumbles, then throws his arms in the air in exasperation, 'I mean, how on earth can we communicate with them Anne?' Still there is no reply. The dog lifts his ear at the change of tone in his master's voice.

Geoffrey stands in front of the fire and flexes his back as much as it will go, which is not very far. The dog gets up on all fours and stretches out the length of his spine, right down to his front paws.

'They will come here bringing with them all sorts of germs, and disgusting habits,' Geoffrey says to the newscaster on the television. The dog gives his right ear a good scratch, then collapses on his backside, rolls over and begins to lick his testicles.

Geoffrey reaches for the television control, points it at his television and presses the off button in a resolute gesture. 'Enough,' he says. 'Walkies Rolo?'

Rolo stands up, shakes himself down, then pads off to the back door, his claws click-clacking on the parquet.

'I'll be back in twenty Anne,' Geoffrey shouts. He stands for a moment, waiting for an answer, then hobbles after his dog.

Anne hears the sound of the back door shutting. She turns off her radio and comes down from her room.

Ballet

Stuart Condie

Here Martin was again, at Annette's party, very smooth operator but not flashy. The music was too loud for conversation, so some of us danced; Martin improvised the ostrich-like moves from *Walk Like an Egyptian*, flicking me a sideways glance to check I was watching.

I'd first spotted him across a blur of faces in the office canteen. It was that New Romantic look with close cropped temples and a large quiff that many tried but few carried off. He fancied himself.

'Martin works in Claims,' my friend Sonia had told me later at the tea urn queue. 'He's got quite a future apparently,' she'd added, examining her nail varnish for flaws.

'Let's talk outside,' Martin now shouted, hot breath and lager in my ear. We stepped over some bodies and opened the French windows onto the paved patio. The garden was all grass and fencing panels, neat but sterile.

'Fag?' he said with a cheeky grin, shaking open his packet of Marlboros. I took one just for the sake of it, but before we had a chance to light up, a slow dance came on, something that jolted me back to college discos in the seventies and my never quite ending up with the right boy. I put my arms around his neck and he took my waist but with light hands, standing afar.

'Can we talk about Sonia?' he murmured as we slowly gyrated around the patio. 'She's pregnant,' Martin added, like he was talking about the weather.

I dropped my hands and stared at him.

'Does your Dad know someone . . . being a GP like?'

His request hung mid-air like the stink of drains in summer; how did he know about my Dad and why did he think . . . the questions piled up like corpses.

Next thing I was rubbing the sting of the slap onto my jeans whilst Martin looked askance, his quiff collapsed.

'Take her to a clinic,' I hissed at him, 'if you must.'

Through the Barricades was playing as I returned to the house.

Chickens Argue all the Time

Samantha Munasing

'You know my Winky?'

'What?'

'Y'know, I have a Winky cos I'm a boy, and you have a pussy cos *you* are a girl?'

'So?'

'To have babies, boys put their Winky in the girl's pussy.'

He's always making things up. Thinks he knows stuff.

'What d'you think of that?'

'Mmmm.'

'Bet you didn't know that.'

I jump up off the grass and run towards the house.

'It's a secret,' he screams, 'You can't tell.'

Thathi sits at the dining table drinking tea, the newspaper propped up against the teapot. He's all dressed up for work.

As I reach for the case by Thathi's feet *he* runs in all sweaty and horrible and grabs it.

'Way quicker than you. Fastest gun in the West,' he says and saunters out like *he's* off to work.

I am hot all over. Right in the middle of my chest there is pain.

'He said,' I say to Thathi,' he said that boys put their Winky into girls. That *you* put your Winky . . . and . . . all sorts . . . I . . . can't even tell you . . .'

Thathi's face is reddy brown. My pain is worse now. He pushes the cup away and leaves the room and returns soon with the Pain Cane and Ammi. Her face is fallen. I run all the way down the garden to the chicken house and huddle behind it. Chickens argue all the time, quite loud.

Later, I peer through the half-opened door to my brother's room. He is on the bed, on his tummy. Ammi gazes down at his bare bottom and the backs of his legs and murmur soft words. At last I think he sleeps. Ammi comes out of the room and looks down at me. She seems so far away. I see raised red marks on her hands, swabs of cotton wool clutched in her fingers. Some are pink. We look at each other for a moment and then she says, 'Don't disturb your brother,' and walks away. 'I didn't mean to,' I want to say, but my voice doesn't come out.

Ted and Moira

Danielle Sensier

Everyone commented on how much Ted was taken with her and looking back, Moira wonders if that's why she said yes.

Friends and family egged them on, hungry for happy endings; it was after the war, and here was a man, saved, whole, and determined to have her.

In their wedding picture the couple stand at the door to St Swithun's, hands clasped, shoulders slightly apart. Ted wears a borrowed morning suit, Moira a single white gardenia pinned to her gown. For several years, she had only to close her eyes to recall the scent.

And then for an even longer time she managed to forget it.

Until now, in this room, where Moira waits, all the last necessities of life - bags to be changed, fluids measured, pills taken - filling the air with a muddy sweetness that summons it back again.

She looks at her watch.

Outside, the sun is setting. From her chair, she can track its progress through the bedroom curtains that for fifty years or more, never quite met in the middle.

Folding the crisp white sheet under Ted's chin and over his arms, she reaches for his hand, tracing the feathery skin with its swollen veins and liver spots, and is rewarded with an answering flutter, less certain than a week ago. She gets up, stretches her neck from side to side and rolls back her shoulders.

Tomorrow, another woman - the nurse with the name she can't pronounce - will take her place for an hour or two. The woman is efficient; she can sit for long periods of time without speaking, her sensible shoes, with the rubber soles and the white laces, planted firmly on the bedroom carpet, unmoving.

When she comes, Moira will go for a walk along the promenade. She'll wear her best coat and shoes and if there's rain, she'll carry an umbrella.

Dream

Judith Bruce

Logs crackled cheerfully in the log-burner and the sofa was comfortable. Morgan switched the table-lamp on and a golden glow enveloped them.

'Nice place you got here, Morg,' said Keith, sitting on the sofa next to him, shoes kicked off, feet extended to the blaze.

'You got a hole in one of them socks,' said Morgan.

'Yeah,' said Keith, leaning forward to examine it. 'Ne'mind, eh?'

Morgan put his head back on the cushions behind him. Music was playing softly - Billie Holliday '*I fall to pieces . . .*' This 'streaming' stuff was tops.

'Got any whisky, Morg, ole mate? asked Keith.

'Soda or water?' he asked as he got up.

'Neat old pal,' said Keith.

Morgan was at the side table, pouring whisky from a cut-glass decanter into two tumblers.

'Yeah - why dilute the good stuff, eh?' He handed Keith his glass and sat down again beside him with a sigh, taking a swig of whisky. 'Good, all this, doncha think?' He waved a hand round his sitting room - fitted carpet, lined curtains, polished dining-table - old style, but pukka.

'Didn't half have a funny dream last night, though,' he added.

'Go on,' said Keith sipping his whisky.

'Awful it was,' said Morgan. 'I was out sleeping on the freezing streets under Waterloo Bridge. Lost me job, couldn't pay the mortgage, lost the cottage, lost the lot.'

'Cor - bloody nightmare,' observed Keith.

A log slipped and sparks flew.

'Yeah - but it happens, though,' said Morgan, draining his glass.

He leant back on the cushions once more but found them hard. And cold. And wet.

'Come on mate,' said a voice, 'you can't sleep 'ere. 'go and find a shelter or something. There's one round the corner.'

A torch was shining into his face and the copper was shaking him. 'You've got to move, both of you.'

Keith was a hump under a sleeping bag next to him. Waterloo Bridge loomed above them.

Triumph and Tribulation

Jayne Block

The sun blazed at the end of the long desert road. Soon it would set and I would still be here, as the darkness fell and the temperatures followed. My only companion for the night - my most cherished possession, my Triumph motorcycle, with its glossy black tank and its hi-shine chrome.

She was more than just an object; she was an adventure, a lifestyle, a thrill, and a temptress. At least she was, until the electrics died. I sighed and looked around for shelter. There was none.

I came on this trip to 'find myself', as the saying goes. Well, there sure as heck wasn't anyone else out here, except maybe bobcats or even bandits, whom I sincerely hoped wouldn't find me. I took out my last bottle of water and sipped it slowly.

After an hour of praying for help, meditating to quell the rising panic and wishing I had stayed at home, I searched for my emergency pack of cigarettes. I wasn't smoking much these days, but if I was going to die out here then abstinence seemed a bit pointless. The foil inner lining of the packet caught the sun. I looked at the foil, like a magpie, drawn to its metallic gleam. Metal has many properties; it can heat up and not burn; it's a great conductor of electricity.

I pulled the plastic side panel off the bike and took the burnt fuse out of its clamps. I tore off a strip of the foil and wound it round the fuse so that it touched the metal caps at both ends. I put everything back in place.

My hand shook as I turned the key. The dials lit up. I had power. I pressed the start button. The engine rumbled into life.

I whooped for joy and gave the petrol tank a lipstick kiss, slung on my jacket, helmet and gloves, and rode off west into that damned American sunset.

About the Authors

Jayne Block - lives near the South Downs with her husband, children, cats and a horse. She loves riding on the Downs and walking through the fields.

Judith Bruce - worked as a BBC television producer before turning to writing. Her memoir *Funny How Things Turn Out* is published by Simon & Schuster. She lives in Eastbourne and is an enthusiastic blogger.

Stuart Condie - had a successful career in aviation before studying creative writing at Sussex University. Three of his short stories are published, four have won prizes, and he's now concentrating on a novel trilogy.

Yvonne Hennessy - lives in Ditchling with her husband, film-maker Luke Holland; they have two sons. She has worked as a teacher and garden-designer, and enjoys writing, pottery and European travels.

Samantha Munasing - was born in Sri Lanka, and now lives with her husband in Alfriston.

Danielle Sensier - has Mauritian roots, grew up in Yorkshire, and calls Sussex home. Her poems for children are published in various anthologies, and she has recently completed a first novel for adults.